Bugs and Slugs

Judy Tatchell
Designed by Ruth Russell and Jane Rigby
Illustrated by Justine Torode

Buzzzzzz

Bees and wasps

Can you find a bee on this page? It is collecting a sweet liquid called nectar from a flower.

Bees make honey from nectar.

Wasps love sweet things. They are a nuisance if they come after your food.

Wasp

If a wasp or bee is scared, it might sting, so don't try to hit it.

This is a bumble bee. It is looking for nectar.

Is that a bee or a wasp on the peach? Lift the flap to see.

Spiders

Spiders eat flies and other insects. They make sticky webs to catch them in.

Yum yum!

A spider makes a new web each morning.

Spiders have oily feet. These stop them from getting stuck in their webs.

Help!

This fly has just flown into the web.

Worms

Worms break up soil as they burrow. This helps plants push their roots into the soil.

It isn't easy to tell which end of a worm is the front!

A worm moves by stretching out the front of its body.

Front of worm

Back of worm

Then it pulls the back part foward.

Butterflies

Butterflies lay eggs on leaves. Out of each egg comes a tiny caterpillar.

I'm very hungry!

Case

The tiny caterpillar eats the leaves.

It makes a case around itself. Inside, it turns into a butterfly.

After a few
weeks, the
butterfly
comes out
of its case.

It stretches its
wings and flies
away.

Flies

Flies taste through their feet! They walk on things to see if they want to eat them.

It's very hard to swat flies because they whizz around so fast.

If a fly with dirty feet walks on your food, the dirt might make you ill.

If you see a fly near food...

WhizzzzZZZZZZZZZzzzzzz

ZZZZZZZZ

Rod is under here.

The fly's big wings help it to fly quickly.

It has a little rod under each wing which helps it to balance.

A fly's mouth works like a sponge. It soaks up soggy food.

Ladybugs and aphids

Ladybugs are easy to see. You can count their spots.

Ladybugs like to eat aphids. Can you see any aphids?

If the ladybug eats these aphids...

Aphids suck a liquid, called sap, from buds. The buds dry up. A dry bud won't open into a flower.

Ants

Where are these ants going?

When an ant finds food, it leaves a trail for other ants to follow.

We're following a trail to some food...

I'm hungry!

Slugs and snails

Slugs and snails like damp, cool places.

What's eating this lettuce?

Munch Munch

Snails cannot see well, but they are good at smelling and feeling.

Some birds eat snails. They have to break the shell.

I'm safe inside my shell.

Who's at the end of this shiny trail?

If snails and slugs dry out, they can't make slime.

A snail's shell helps stop it from drying out in the sun.

Beetles

Beetles like to live among leaves and sticks. They eat tiny insects.

Wing case

A beetle has two hard, shiny wing cases over its wings. These keep its wings safe.

Wing case

When a beetle flies, it holds its wing cases out of the way.

Centipedes and millipedes

A centipede is very wriggly. It eats smaller creatures. It has to run quickly to catch its food.

Centipede

A millipede eats plants. It cannot run as fast as a centipede, but it has more legs!

Millipede

Whose tail is this?

First published in 1999 by Usborne Publishing Ltd, Usborne House, 83-85 Saffron Hill, London EC1N 8RT, England.
www.usborne.com
Copyright © Usborne Publishing Ltd, 1999. First published in America 1999. AE

Printed in Singapore.